Olive's Treasure

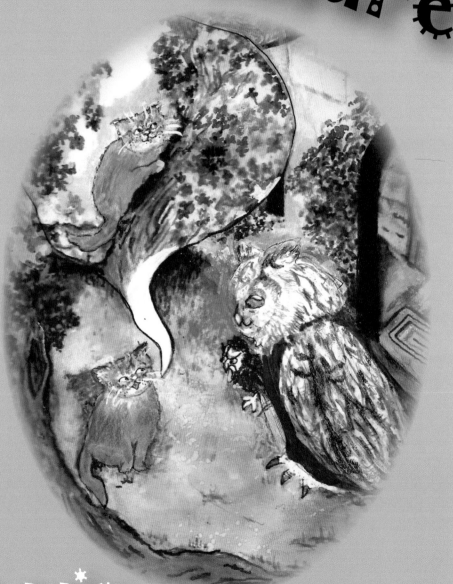

Maggie Alexander

In the
old tree house
not a sound
could be heard.
Not a whisper.
Not a murmur.
Not a giggle.
Not a word.

3

No little wings.
No little beaks.
No little feathers
tickling cheeks.
Olive woke up
and she was
alone...

5

her children to other
nests had flown.

Olive was sipping
her morning tea
and dunking her biscuits
one, two,
three.
She heard a strange sound
from outside the house
—a squirrel, perhaps,
or even a mouse?
"I'll have a fourth biscuit
and a bit more tea
and then I'd better go
and see."

She was on her sixth biscuit
and her third teacup
when the peculiar sound
made her get up.
A mewing, scratching,
sound from above.
Could it be blackbirds,
a robin, a dove?

11

She put down her tea
and went through the door.
She looked to the roof
and heard it some more.
A squeaking, scrabbling,
yowling sound.
Then something orange
fell to the ground.
Olive could scarcely believe
her eyes.
"It's a kitten!"
she exclaimed in surprise.

"Meow, meow!"

said the orange ball.
"I climbed quite easily
onto the wall
and then began
to climb quite high
until I was nearly
in the sky.
I couldn't get down.
My claws won't grip.
I could feel myself begin to slip....

then I seemed
to fly through the air
and now I'm here,
I don't know where!"

"You're in my garden," Olive replied.
"I think you better come inside."

The orange ball began to weep
and lay on the table
in a crumpled heap.

18

The orange ball's cries got stronger.
"I don't have a home
any longer!
The family I lived with moved away
and left me with no place to stay."

"I myself am all alone
now my children all have flown.
If you like you could stay with me?
Stop your crying
and have some tea."

"What's your name?
You're not called Cat.
I can't continue to call you that!"

"Mostly I was called
Meow or Thing or Pest.
Meow was probably the best."

"Meow is not a name." she cried.
"Or Pest or Thing, but what?"
she sighed. "What about...

Whiskers,

Tiger,

or Harry?

Silky,

Fluffy,

or Larry?"

The orange ball
sat on Olive's knee.
His mouth was full
of biscuits and tea.

"To have a cat is such a pleasure
His name should be a thing to treasure.

I know what will be your name;

Biscuit
for the day
you came!"

"I like Biscuit
and Biscuit likes me,
so, we'll live together
in the old oak tree."

For Elizabeth "Bib", with love.

FIRST EDITION

Paperback ISBN: 978-1-80227-228-4

eBook ISBN: 978-1-80227-229-1

Printed in Great Britain
by Amazon